Redwood Bear and the Crash! Boom! THUNDERY DAY

by Justine Korman
based on a story by Tina Wilcox

Illustrated by Carol Nicklaus

TARGET. mervyn's

Random House New York

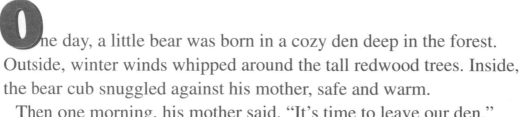

One day, a little bear was born in a cozy den deep in the forest. Outside, winter winds whipped around the tall redwood trees. Inside, the bear cub snuggled against his mother, safe and warm.

Then one morning, his mother said, "It's time to leave our den."

Once outdoors, the little bear blinked in the sudden sunshine. His soft fur glowed like gold in the bright light.

His mother could hardly believe her eyes. "Your fur isn't black or brown, like most bears. It's golden, like the afternoon sun on a redwood tree. I think I'll call you…Redwood!"

But the little cub wasn't listening. He felt afraid. "Mama, why do we have to leave our den?" he asked.

Redwood's mother smiled. "Because my instinct tells me it's time," she said.

"Instinct? What's that?" Redwood asked.

His mother struggled to explain. "Instinct is a voice deep inside each of us. It tells us things such as when we're thirsty and how to find water. Instinct tells a mother how to care for her cub. And my instinct tells me it's time for you to learn and explore!"

Redwood soon found he liked exploring. The world outside his cozy den was full of interesting plants and animals.

"See, hear, smell, taste, and feel!" his mother urged. "Learn as much as you can. Knowledge can keep you safe, and it can help you find important things, like food."

"Listen to your instinct, and you'll always know what to do," his mother said.

Redwood listened. He heard his stomach growl.

His mother laughed. "That's your tummy telling you you're hungry. Now let your instinct lead you to food."

Redwood's mother sniffed the air with her big black nose. Redwood sniffed, too. He smelled honey! Redwood followed his nose to the sweet, sticky snack.

Before long, Redwood was finding streams by their noisy babbling and guessing the weather by the feel of the wind. But there was more to learn. "Instinct will also tell you when danger is near, and what to do," Mama said. "Always listen to your—"

"Instinct," Redwood finished for her. He had learned his lesson well. Now he felt ready to go out on his own.

Mama's instinct told her Redwood was ready, too. All cubs must learn to live on their own someday. At first, Mama worried about sending her sweet golden cub off on his own. But she knew Redwood's instinct would guide him.

Redwood had a great time! He felt very grown-up exploring on his own. First he found some ripe berries, which he gobbled down for lunch. Then he met three bunnies playing hippety-hop. How silly they seemed!

"I'm Holly!" cried the first.

"I'm Berry!" cried the second.

"And I'm Merry!" squeaked the smallest.

"We're going to a clover patch just past this meadow. Would you like to come, too?" Holly asked.

"That's nice of you," Redwood said. "Maybe another time."

The bunnies waved good-bye and went hippety-hop on their way.

As soon as the bunnies were gone, Redwood felt lonely. *Maybe I should have gone with them*, he thought. But something had told Redwood not to go. His tummy felt…jumpy.

Redwood looked up at the sky, which had suddenly turned dark and cloudy. He heard birds returning to their nests and saw a mouse scurrying toward its hole. Yes. It was going to rain. Redwood could almost smell the coming storm on the chill wind.

Redwood listened harder. Underneath the wind, he could hear a voice from deep inside him. The voice said that this would be no ordinary rain. This would be a *dangerous* rain.

Redwood was so scared he almost cried. He wished he was safe with his mother in their den. But then his mother's advice echoed in his mind: *Listen to your instinct, and you'll always know what to do.*

Redwood listened hard. His instinct told him to find shelter. The little cub looked all around. He spotted a cave. *I'll be safe and dry there,* Redwood thought. He ran toward the cave as fast as his chubby legs would carry him.

BOOM! CRASH! FLASH! Huge flashing lights pierced the sky. Great booming sounds seemed to shake the earth. Redwood ran faster toward the cave.

Suddenly he stopped short. Holly, Berry, and Merry were crouched under a big tree. Their fur was soaked, and they looked scared.

Redwood had seen branches fall during a storm. He knew the bunnies shouldn't be sitting under the tree. So he picked them up in his strong paws and carried them to the cave.

And that was a good thing, too! Because just as Redwood and the bunnies entered the cave, lightning struck the big tree. FLASH! CRASH! BOOM!

Redwood and the bunnies stayed together in the dry cave. Being with friends made the storm seem less scary.

When the storm was over, the animals stepped outside. The air was so fresh! Every leaf sparkled.

"Hey, you!"

Redwood heard a loud voice. He looked around, but no one was in sight.

"Up here!" the voice shouted.

At last, Redwood spotted a tiny red bird, who chirped, "I'm Scout. Smooth rescue! Those hippety-hops would've been *through*— if not for you."

"Ah…it was nothing," Redwood said modestly.

"Not according to my boss, Mother Nature. She wants to see you right away," Scout said. "Come on!"

Scout led Redwood through the forest, chattering all the way. He told Redwood how to find a running stream of water and where to catch the best fish. Scout even knew which animals lived where, and how to make a trail.

Redwood was amazed that the tiny bird knew so much! When Scout stopped speaking for a moment, Redwood asked, "What was all that booming and flashing and crashing about?"

Scout laughed. "You mean the thunder and lightning," he said. Then he whipped out a board that had the words *thunder* and *lightning* written on it. "Scary, aren't they?" he added.

Redwood nodded.

"Actually, thunder and lightning aren't so scary once you know what they are. Thunder is just a very loud noise made by air moving very fast," Scout said.

"Why is the air in such a hurry?" Redwood asked.

Scout smiled. "Because it suddenly got very hot when the lightning bolt passed through it."

"Where did the lightning bolt come from?" asked Redwood.

"From inside a cloud," the little bird replied. "Clouds are made up of tiny drops of water and specks of dust swirling through the air. When more and more water droplets gather, the cloud becomes so heavy that all the water falls down to the ground. That's what we call rain."

Redwood was still confused. "But how did the lightning bolt get inside the cloud?"

"Scientists still aren't sure!" Scout exclaimed. "Thunderclouds are very tall. They often have what's called a negative charge at the bottom and a positive one at the top. If the winds are right, these negative and positive charges rub against each other and make electricity. That's the flash we call lightning. Sometimes the lightning strikes the ground, or something tall, like a tree."

Redwood had many more questions. But they had reached the dazzling field of daylilies where Mother Nature waited.

The little cub had never seen anyone so beautiful! Even her dress was alive with blossoms. Her eyes were like stars. Her voice sounded like a soft breeze.

"You are a hero, Redwood Bear," she said. "Because you listened to your instinct, you saved three bunnies—and yourself! You are a smart cub, and I have an important job for you.

"Nature is beautiful, but it is also strong and even, sometimes, dangerous. Children need to understand nature and how to protect themselves from dangers like today's storm."

"But what can I do?" Redwood asked. "I don't know anything about the forces of nature. How can I teach children something I don't know myself?"

Mother Nature smiled and tied a colorful scarf around Redwood's neck. Then she placed a matching hat on his head. "You don't have to know. You just have to be ready to learn," she said.

"He's certainly curious enough for that!" Scout exclaimed.

"And you're chatty enough to teach him," Mother Nature teased. Then she turned to the cub. "Don't worry, Redwood. Scout is a very smart bird. He'll always be around to help you."

Scout's tiny chest puffed with pride.

Just then, Redwood looked up. An arc of every color gently moved
across the sky. Redwood gasped. "How beautiful!" he said.
"It's a rainbow," Scout said.
"What's a rainbow?" Redwood asked.
Scout chuckled. "That's another story!"